WELCOME

Collect the special coins in this book.
You will earn one gold coin for
every chapter you read.

Once you have finished all the chapters,
find out what to do with your gold coins at
the back of the book.

With special thanks to Jasmine Richards

To Jaiden McGilvery, a hero in the making!

www.beastquest.co.uk

ORCHARD BOOKS

First published in Great Britain in 2016 by The Watts Publishing Group

1 3 5 7 9 10 8 6 4 2

Text © 2016 Beast Quest Limited.
Cover and inside illustrations by Steve Sims
© Beast Quest Limited 2016

Beast Quest is a registered trademark of Beast Quest Limited
Series created by Beast Quest Limited, London

A CIP catalogue record for this book is available from the British Library.

ISBN 978 1 40834 086 8

Printed and bound by CPI Group (UK) Ltd, Croydon, CR0 4YY

The paper and board used in this book are made from wood from responsible sources

Orchard Books
An imprint of Hachette Children's Group
Part of The Watts Publishing Group Limited
Carmelite House, 50 Victoria Embankment, London EC4Y 0DZ

An Hachette UK Company
www.hachette.co.uk
www.hachettechildrens.co.uk

KRYTOR
THE BLOOD BAT

BY ADAM BLADE

ORCHARD

VILLAGE

KING
HUGO'S
PALACE

KARIXA'S MIN

TRIAL OF HEROES

JUNGLE

CORSAIR ISLAND

CONTENTS

A great battle has just taken place in Avantia. The City was almost destroyed by a raging Beast, and many lives were at risk...

Thankfully, a courageous warrior came to our aid, and peace was restored to the capital. But this warrior was not Tom, nor was it Elenna, for they were across the ocean, fighting bravely on another Quest. Now Avantia has a new champion, laying claim to Tom's title of Master of the Beasts.

And this courageous fighter has an honest claim to that title, which means there is only one thing for it.

Tom must put his title on the line. He and his opponent must complete the Trial of Heroes.

May the bravest warrior win.

Aduro, former wizard to King Hugo

HOME!

"Ouch!" Elenna yelped, hopping onto one foot. "I've got a stone in my boot!"

Tom grinned as he watched his friend retrieve the stone and hurl it away.

"Just a little pebble," he said, pleased to have a moment to rest. "I can't believe you're complaining so much. We've been through worse."

"A lot worse." Elenna laughed. "Why couldn't Daltec magic us back from Gwildor?"

She has a point, Tom thought. The journey back to Avantia had been long and gruelling, taking them over both land and sea.

Tom lifted his chin. Being a Master of the Beasts meant doing difficult things. This journey home was just part of that. He pointed up ahead at the soaring towers of King Hugo's palace in the City. "Look, not that far now."

"Then what are waiting for?" Elenna winced as she strode forwards. "I really do need to get my boots mended. Right now, they have more holes than they do leather."

Tom smiled again, but it was forced. Elenna's footwear wasn't the only thing that needed mending. His fingers crept to the shield that hung from his side. It had not been the same since the Beast Thoron's lightning struck it. The battle-scarred wood was rough beneath his fingertips, and the tokens that studded the shield were cool to the touch. They had been drained of colour and their powers still had not returned.

"I'm sure Aduro or Daltec will be able to fix your shield," Elenna said, watching Tom closely.

"I hope so," Tom murmured.

"What are you looking forward to most about being home?" Elenna asked after a moment.

Tom could tell that she was trying to take his mind off things.

"A warm bath," Tom said. "And a soft bed. It will be nice to sleep and not worry about being on a Quest just for—"

"Wait, can you smell that?" Elenna interrupted. "It's smoke."

Tom sniffed. His friend was right. He ran forward, taking the twisty road at a sprint. *People might be in danger!*

Tom and Elenna rounded the bend and were faced with the remains of a charred wagon on the road. Its cover

was completely scorched and the
wheels were just blackened stumps.
Crates, upturned baskets and rotting
fruit and vegetables were strewn

over the road but there didn't appear to be any people in sight.

Elenna poked at a charred apple with her toe. "Looks like some market traders were on the way to the City when the wagon caught fire."

"There are no wounded or dead, though," Tom said. "Everyone escaped."

He continued to scan the scene of the accident. There were scorch-marks up and down the path but they appeared as patches rather than as a trail of fire. *How odd. How did the fire start in the first place?* he wondered. *And why was it allowed to do so much damage without someone trying to stop it?*

Tom looked further up the path and saw more patches of ash on the ground, with swathes of vegetation burned away on either side. "Elenna, something is not right about this."

His friend nodded. "Let's get to the City. We might get some answers there."

They quickened their pace, and soon arrived at the city gates.

"Halt!" a soldier at the entrance said.

"Greetings. I am Tom, Master of the Beasts and protector of Avant—"

The soldier snorted. "I know who you are."

Tom paused. He wasn't expecting a great fanfare. After all, news probably hadn't come yet from Gwildor of their successes in the previous Quests. Still, he normally got along with Captain Harkman's troops.

Tom looked at the other soldiers on the gate. They were all scowling at him.

"Do we have a problem here?" Elenna asked, hands on hips.

"I'd say so." The first soldier waved them towards the gate irritably. "It's way past time the Master of the Beasts turned up."

Tom frowned as they turned grudgingly to open the gates. The soldier seemed angry at him. But why?

As the gates swung open, a flurry of red and orange filled his vision. It was Epos the Flame Bird, in the middle of the courtyard beyond! The Good Beast was in chains, thrashing on the ground. A manacle encircled her long elegant neck and steel chains bound her mighty wings.

Tom ran forward and drew his sword ready to sever her bonds. As he did so, Epos let out a pitiful keen, almost as if she was scared of him.

Tom lowered his sword, anger making him shake. *Poor Epos*, he thought as he approached her. *She no longer knows who is friend or foe.*

Elenna was running right by his side, her face determined. As they got nearer to Epos, a throng of soldiers formed ranks around the flame bird.

"Let me through," Tom demanded.

"I'm Master of the Beasts."

"No one is to go near the Beast under pain of death," one of the soldiers said. "King Hugo's orders."

Tom's fingers tightened on his

sword but Elenna shook her head.

"Fighting is not the answer," she said.
"We should speak to King Hugo and
find out what's going on."

Tom nodded but, first, he wanted

to hear what Epos had to say. He sheathed his sword, then called on the power of his red jewel and tried to form a connection with the Beast. But all he could sense was confusion.

I'll come back for you, Epos, Tom vowed. *Right after I get some answers.*

He and Elenna strode to King Hugo's throne room, the soldiers on the door knowing better than to get in the Master of the Beast's way. Tom threw open the heavy doors with a crash. King Hugo sat on his throne with Aduro by his side.

The king and his former wizard halted their conversation as Tom and Elenna entered the throne room. It was only Daltec, the young wizard, who jumped to his feet in delight. "Tom! Elenna! You're back!"

Tom crossed his arms. "Why has Epos been chained up? She's a Good Beast!"

King Hugo frowned and Tom could tell he was not pleased by the criticism.

Aduro held up a soothing hand.

"Tom, much has happened since you've been away." The lines in the wizard's face looked deeper than before. "Epos went berserk. She destroyed many homes, and endangered the life of Avantian citizens."

"No, I can't believe that," Tom said.

Aduro spread his arms wide. "Without you here, we didn't know what to do. Thankfully, a hero came forward."

"A hero?" Tom repeated.

"That would be me," a voice said from behind them.

Tom and Elenna turned around. Standing in the doorway was a figure dressed in full golden armour that Tom knew as well as the shield he wore on his arm. The figure was tall and carried a double-bladed battle-axe.

"My Golden Armour!" Tom exclaimed.

"Not any more." The figure removed the helmet to reveal a girl of about

sixteen years of age, with long blonde
hair that tumbled free. She smirked.
"It's a good fit, isn't it?"

A NEW RIVAL

"Tom, Elenna, this is Amelia," Aduro
said. "She's been a great help to the
kingdom whilst you've been gone,
but we have missed you."

Tom couldn't speak. His words had
dried up.

"I don't care what this pretender's
name is," Elenna snapped. "Only
a Master or Mistress of the Beasts

should wear the Golden Armour."

"Quite right, Eleanor." Amelia strode into the middle of the chamber. "Good thing I am a Mistress of the Beasts."

"Her name is Elenna, not Eleanor," Tom said, finding his voice. "And just because you say you're a Mistress of the Beasts doesn't mean you are one." He glared at her. "You've stolen that armour – and that battle-axe isn't yours, either. It belongs in the Gallery of Tombs."

Amelia twirled the battle-axe in her hand, the blade becoming a whirlwind of sharp metal. "Careful, I don't like your tone." She laughed. "I'd threaten to cut you down to size

but you're pretty short already.
I really thought you'd be bigger."

Tom reached for his sword.

"Enough," King Hugo demanded. "Both of you stand down." He made a steeple of his fingers. "I know it might be difficult for you to accept, Tom, but Amelia came to our rescue and vanquished Epos before anyone was killed. We – and you – owe her a debt of thanks."

Tom took a deep breath. He did not want to be disrespectful to the king but the truth needed to be told. "Sire, of course I am grateful that no one got hurt, but Amelia shouldn't have the armour. She's not a Mistress of the Beasts."

"That isn't exactly true." Aduro leaned wearily on his staff as he stood. "Amelia is a descendant of

Kara and, as you know, Kara was Mistress of the Beasts when I was an apprentice." Aduro pointed at the weapon in Amelia's hand. "The battle-axe that belonged to Kara is Amelia's birthright. Also, the laws of the kingdom allow anyone to lay claim to the title of Master or Mistress of the Beasts."

"But there can't be two." Tom hated how unsure his voice sounded.

"I'm sorry, Tom, but I have consulted the Chronicles and there is nothing to be done about it," Daltec said. "This has happened before – several times, in fact – but not for over a hundred years."

"And what happened?" Elenna

demanded. "How was a decision reached?"

"In the case of two candidates vying for the title of Master or Mistress of the Beasts, both must pass a test to prove who is most worthy of the honour," Daltec replied.

"Have I not proven myself already?" Tom asked. "Elenna and I have saved this kingdom and others from destruction more times than I can count."

"I can tell," Amelia said. "You both sound really tired – and you look a state." She shrugged. "Maybe it's time to retire?"

Tom ignored her. "Tell me about

the test, Daltec."

"It's called the Trial of Heroes," the young wizard explained. "Each candidate must face four Beasts, and retrieve the Rune of Courage. Whoever triumphs is crowned Master or Mistress of the Beasts."

"Wait a moment," Elenna said. "What happens to the loser?"

Daltec paled. "I cannot lie to you, Elenna. More often than not neither candidate comes back to claim the title."

"This is ridiculous," Tom said. "I can't allow Amelia to get herself killed."

"It sounds like you're scared." Amelia was smirking again. "Just say now if you're too frightened to do the trial. I know I'm ready."

"It is clear that Amelia is willing to accept the terms of the trial." Daltec looked over at Tom, his expression anxious. "I hate to say it, but it seems as though it's the only way. What is your decision?"

Tom couldn't quite believe that any of this was really happening. He glanced over at Elenna. She looked as confused and hurt as he felt. He swallowed. There was no way he could allow Amelia to steal his title. There was only one possible answer he could give. He nodded. "I accept."

"So be it," Daltec said. "You

and Amelia may both choose a companion to take on your Quest."

"I choose Elenna," Tom said immediately. "If she wants to come."

"Of course I do," Elenna said. "And we'll succeed in this test like we have with all others."

"We'll see about that." Amelia snorted. "I'll take my uncle, Dray."

From the shadows in the corner of the room, a figure silently appeared. Tom couldn't believe that he hadn't noticed the man before. He was almost seven feet tall, with grey skin and a bald head. He must have been standing as still as a sculpture to have gone unnoticed. Even now he was in the light, Dray

didn't appear to blink.

"I'll fetch the maps that will help you complete the trial." Daltec strode towards the door, his robes billowing out behind him. "We'll meet in the courtyard below."

"Good, because I have unfinished business there." Tom looked over at King Hugo. "I need to free Epos."

"That's madness," Amelia cried. "The Beast is a danger to—"

"Sire," Tom interrupted, "if my service to the kingdom and my previous Quests mean anything to you, then please let me free the Good Beast."

King Hugo nodded once. "If you think it is safe for Epos to be released then I trust your judgement. Aduro?"

"I agree," the former wizard said. "Tom is wiser than his years and will always make the right choice. Good luck, my young friend – with everything."

"Thank you." Tom bowed and then

hurried from the chamber, Elenna right behind him. As he raced down the stairs, Tom realised that Amelia and Dray were also following. The man with the grey skin moved swiftly despite his size and the large broadsword that hung from his side.

They spilt out into the courtyard. "Stand aside," Tom commanded, staring at Epos behind the wall of soldiers. The flame bird's eyes were closed and her normally vibrant feathers looked dul. Tom felt a wave of frustration as he realised that his sword was not strong enough to cut through the chains.

"On whose orders?" a soldier cried.

"Mine," Captain Harkman barked,

appearing next to Tom. The soldiers melted away at their commander's voice.

Tom focused on the red jewel in his belt, willing his voice to cut through the confusion that clouded the Beast's mind. *Spread your wings, Epos. Break the chains that bind you.*

The flame bird remained still for a moment, then she threw back her head and let out a high-pitched cry. Spreading her wings to their full span, she flapped upwards and snapped the chains.

As she rose into the sky, Tom spotted some kind of metal barb digging into her flank.

What is that? he wondered, but

before he could get another look, her feathers burst into beautiful flames and he could see no more. Epos soared up and up, only to be jerked back to the ground by the manacle that was still attached to her neck.

Wait, Tom said, using the red jewel again. *You must stay calm or you'll hurt yourself.*

Epos lowered herself to the ground and the flames that had lit up her feathers faded.

Tom took his chance and had a closer look at the metal barb that was lodged in the flame bird's side. Tugging it free, he saw that it was some kind of dart. The metal barb was hollow and a few drops of green liquid leaked from its tip.

"What is that thing?" Elenna asked.

"A poisoned dart," Tom said. "I think that is why Epos has been acting so strangely."

Elenna gasped. "Who would do such a cruel thing?"

"I don't know," Tom replied. "But if they are an enemy of Epos, they are an enemy of mine."

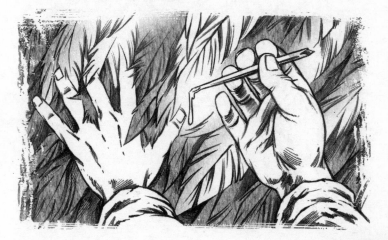

THE QUEST BEGINS

How do you feel, Epos? Tom asked.

I feel ashamed, the Beast said mournfully. Her voice was much clearer now the effects of the poison had worn off. *Why have I acted like this?*

It's not your fault, Tom explained. *You were poisoned.* He looked over at the group of soldiers. "I'll need the key for the last of the chains."

There was a murmur of annoyance but then the key was tossed to him. Tom caught it and then carefully removed the manacle from around Epos's neck.

Thank you, the Beast said, rising into the sky once more. She let out a mighty shriek, and then she was gone, gliding away on the air.

"How touching," Amelia said, coming to stand by his side. "You've just released a murderous bird back into the wild. I'm sure everyone in Avantia will be most grateful." She shook her head. "That Beast needed to be slain."

Tom forced himself to take a deep breath. The idea of anyone hurting

Epos made him feel sick. "You have a lot to learn about being a Mistress of the Beasts," Tom replied. "The job means you work with the Beasts – you don't just mindlessly kill them."

They were interrupted by Daltec, who had arrived in the courtyard. "I have the maps. So now you must get ready for your Quest." He pointed at Amelia. "Remove the armour. And Tom, give me your jewelled belt."

"Why?" Amelia demanded.

"Because both of you must face the trial without magical assistance," Daltec explained. "And you must also leave behind any animal companions."

"Fine," Amelia said, shrugging off

her armour. "I don't need a hunk of
metal to win this contest."

"And I don't need my belt or
its powers to be victorious." Tom
handed over the length of leather,
studded with its magic jewels, to
Daltec. He was pleased his voice

didn't betray how lost he would feel without his belt and the magical abilities it gave him.

"Then let us begin," the young wizard said. He gave them both a rolled-up parchment. "Both of these are maps of the Nowhere Lands. It is here that the trial will take place."

"The Nowhere Lands," Tom repeated. "I've never heard of it."

Daltec looked grim. "Neither had I, until I started doing research about the trial. But it is where you must go." Reaching into the fold of his robes, the young wizard removed a phial of oily, black liquid. Smoke swirled from the top of it as he removed the stopper. Chanting

softly, Daltec poured the liquid
directly onto the ground.

Tom watched as the fluid cut
through the flagstones of the
courtyard and opened up a hole

into blackness. The hole got wider and wider, until it stretched several paces. A cold wind whipped out of the abyss and howled in his ears.

Daltec turned to face Tom, Amelia, Elenna and Dray. "Farewell," the young wizard said. "Please step into the darkness."

Tom saw Amelia swallow hard. If he hadn't known better, he'd have said that the older girl looked scared.

Amelia nodded her head at Dray. "You go first."

Tom was surprised to see the girl's uncle obey without question. He stepped off the edge of the abyss and vanished. Amelia took a running jump after him and also disappeared.

Tom turned to Elenna. "You don't have to come with me," he said. "There's no duty involved this time."

"Stop being ridiculous," Elenna replied. She grabbed his arm and together they jumped into the void.

Cold air screamed past Tom's ears and stung his eyes as he fell through the blackness. He called out Elenna's name but the word was swallowed by the wind.

He didn't know how long he fell for but he finally felt something solid beneath his feet, and light flooded over him. Staring out, he saw that he was on the edge of a vast, desert-like tundra. Elenna was at his side, blinking in the bright daylight.

Dray and Amelia were standing
a few feet away from them on the
edge of the black abyss, the wind
snatching at their clothing. The black
hole was shrinking away to nothing.
No turning back now, Tom thought,
but Amelia wasn't even watching.
She had her back to Tom, and was
fiddling with something he couldn't
see, while Dray held their map.

Tom took out his own map and
surveyed it, taking in the rocky paths
and mountain ranges.

"Let's go," said Amelia. She then
whipped around to face Tom. "Stay
out of my way, little boy, or you
might get hurt."

"Worry about yourself, not us,"

Elenna shot back. "Tom and I have completed more Quests than you've had hot dinners."

"We'll see." Amelia smirked and strode away with her uncle.

Elenna's hands clenched into fists. "That girl really annoys me."

"I know," Tom said. "But like you said, we've completed many Quests and we know what we have to do." He looked down again at their map and saw that there was a red dot, like a spot of blood, that hadn't been there before. A name was inscribed beneath it in curling, elaborate script: *KRYTOR*.

Tom tapped the parchment. "This must be the first Beast on the trial."

He frowned. "But Amelia's gone in completely the wrong direction."

"That's her problem," Elenna said. "Come on, we'll get a head start."

"You're right," Tom said. *And this way at least Amelia can be kept out of danger.* He shook his head. *She's not going to do very well on this Quest if she can't even read a map.*

A heat haze shimmered in the air as Tom and Elenna set out across the dusty landscape. The sun beat down relentlessly on them. The ground was not as flat as it first seemed. It rose and fell as they walked, the surface shifting beneath their feet.

"We need to get out of this sun." Elenna's voice was scratchy and dry.

Tom pointed over to a nearby bluff. "Look, there's a small cave opening up there. It will give us shade."

They clambered up the rocky path and arrived in the cool, shadowy interior. "That's better." Elenna's voice echoed around the cave.

It was followed by a strange chattering noise.

Tom's hand crept to his sword as the squeaks got louder and closer. "Something's coming," he said.

Elenna reached for her bow and arrow. "It can't be Krytor, can it? The map says he still far away."

"Maybe it's a trap." Tom held his sword in front of him and squinted into the darkness.

The red glint of hundreds of eyes stared back at him, and his heart began to thump harder.

"Tom, run," Elenna cried.

Too late. A tide of black surged over them.

4

THE EMPTY GRAVE

Tom could feel pricks of pain
all over his body as sharp talons
tore his clothes. Leathery wings
beat at his face and he staggered
backwards, finally realising what
was attacking them.

"Bats!" he cried, as they continued
to swirl all around him. He swung
out with the flat of his sword but the

creatures were far too quick.

"Why are they attacking us?" Elenna cried, her arms flailing. "I thought bats were supposed to be shy."

"Things must be different in the

Nowhere Lands." Tom swung out
with his sword again but it was a
hopeless task. There were too many of
them. He staggered backwards as the
bats drove him out of the cave and
daylight surrounded him. Tom saw
Elenna – eyes wide and her face all
scratched from the claws of the bats –
emerge as well.

"Are you all ri—" Tom began but
broke off as the bats surged at him
again. Stepping backwards he felt the
crumbling edge of the cliff beneath
his feet...and then nothing at all.

Panic robbed Tom of even the
breath to cry out as he fell through
the air. He was falling, tumbling
down some kind of ravine. Out of

instinct, his fingers scrabbled to grab at something, but they just came away with dust and pebbles. He could hear Elenna screaming his name.

He needed to do something. Pushing down his fear, Tom focused on the walls of the ravine. Small, scrubby plants poked out of the rock face here and there, and with a cry he reached out and grabbed one.

The bush was thorny and cut into the skin of his palm, but it was strong, with deep roots. The muscles in his arm screamed in pain as he came to an abrupt halt and was then jerked upwards. Tom hung there, battered and bruised.

A moment later, he saw Elenna

tumbling past. He kicked against the
wall and swung out, using his free
hand to grab her arm. More pain
shot through his shoulder as he took
her weight as well.

"I've got you," he said, as they both dangled over the steep drop and the rocky ground below. He could feel sweat beading on his brow. It was taking all his strength to hold on to his friend.

Elenna swallowed hard. "Thank you, Tom."

"Don't thank me yet." Tom looked up. He could see the swarm of bats spiralling down towards them. "They're not finished with us."

"What are we going to do?"

Tom shook his head as he stared at the approaching black cloud of leathery wings and talons. *I can't believe I'm going to fail the Trial of Heroes before I've even met the first*

Beast. Fury raged through him. Was this really the way it was going to end?

Suddenly, Tom heard a strange, high-pitched whistle and the hovering bats rose up as one and banked away in formation, soon disappearing from sight.

"What was that?" said Elenna.

A moment later, Tom heard a voice from above. "Hold on, let me help you."

Tom looked up to see a young boy on the edge of the ravine. He wore a wooden flute around his neck and was lowering down a thick length of rope.

"Elenna, you'll have to go first," Tom said.

His friend caught the rope with her free hand and looped it under her armpits, even managing to tie a knot.

The boy above them pulled on the rope and Elenna used her feet to kick against the wall and scramble up the rock face.

Tom waited and when the rope came down again, he followed.

The young boy was wide-eyed as Tom came to stand next to him and Elenna on the ledge that sat a few feet beneath the cave where the bats lived.

"You are not from my village," the boy said in wonder.

"No, we are from a kingdom far away," Tom said. "A place called Avantia."

The boy's eyes got even wider and

his mouth stretched into an excited smile. "You're lucky I was close by and could frighten away the bats," he said. "I wasn't sure I'd get to the top of the cliff in time."

"Thank you for saving us," said Elenna. "Was it that flute you used to scare away the bats?"

The boy looked down at his feet. "You'll find out soon enough. Everything will become clear."

Tom and Elenna exchanged a look. *What a strange thing to say.*

"Please, follow," said the boy, turning and walking off.

Tom shrugged. What other choice did they have? He placed a hand around the hilt of his sword, and saw Elenna nod back at him. They would remain ready for anything.

As they found a safe path down from the cliffs, the boy introduced himself as Karil. They found his

small donkey eating some scrappy grass and they re-attached the rope to the animal's harness.

Together they walked to Karil's village. It was made up of lots of domed mud huts, and each of the doorways was marked with the symbol of a bat. As Tom and Elenna walked further into the village, people lined the streets and stared in awe at them. Many bowed their heads. It was strange. *It's almost as if these people know me already and have been waiting for me to arrive,* Tom thought.

A shaman, wearing a necklace of bones, began to chant as they walked past. Coming closer, he placed the

necklace around Tom's neck. He then
whispered something in Karil's ear.

The young boy nodded and they
continued onwards until Tom and
Elenna were brought to a patch of

ground with engraved tablets of
stones planted in it.

A cemetery, Tom realised.

When they reached the middle of
the graveyard, there was a single hole
dug and waiting for a body.

"Look who it is!" Elenna said.

Amelia and Dray were waiting for
them on the other side of the hole.
"Took your time, didn't you?" Amelia
leant against a tombstone.

Tom noticed she was also wearing
a necklace of bones. "What is the
meaning of all this?" he asked.

Karil looked at them sadly. "The
grave," he said, pointing at the hole. "It
is for one of you."

5

THIEF!

"What are you talking about?"
Elenna demanded.

"There is a ritual in our village,"
Karil explained. "We must bear
witness to the battle that takes
place between two warriors and the
bat-Beast that comes from the sky."
The young boy hugged himself as if
cold. "It has not happened for many

generations, but here you are." Karil pointed to the tombstones and Tom could see that they were engraved with unfamiliar names and the symbols of weapons.

"You see, you are not first to come and do battle with the Beast – and you will not be the last."

Tom shuddered. Death had visited this place before. "But I do not wish to bring a Beast to your village," Tom said.

Karil smiled. "My people will be safe. That's why they mark their houses with the sign of the bat. It protects us." Karil held up his flute. "Besides, I have this. It was given to me by my grandfather. He said the flute once belonged to a great warrior who was slain trying to defeat the Beast."

Amelia gave a bark of laughter. "Well, of course he got killed. He should have used a decent sword instead of a whistle." She touched her necklet of bones. "Watch and learn, people. I will kill that Beast even if the witch doctor says it's impossible."

"What are you talking about?" Tom demanded. He hated that Amelia had got to the village first. It felt like she had all the information and he was stumbling around in the dark.

Amelia waved a hand dismissively. "The witch doctor said that Krytor can only be subdued, and not killed. But we'll see about that."

Karil shook his head. "Our shaman is wise. You should heed his words." He beckoned them away from the graveside. "Come, now that both warriors have arrived, Krytor will return to our village – but not until nightfall. The blood bat only comes after dark."

"So, what will we do until then?" Elenna asked.

"You must join us for a meal," Karil responded. "After all, it may be the last thing you ever eat."

"Well, that's a cheering thought," Elenna murmured.

As Tom followed the young boy away from the tombstones, he tried to walk next to Amelia but Dray blocked his way.

"Can you ask your uncle to move?" Tom requested, patiently.

"We need to talk strategy."

Amelia raised an eyebrow but waved Dray away. "Go on, I'm listening."

"We need to team up," Tom said. "Did you see the tombstones? Those warriors ended up dying because they were too busy fighting each other instead of the Beast. Together, we'll defeat Krytor."

"I don't need any help," Amelia said. She strode off with Dray at her side.

"You're wasting your time with her," Elenna said.

The heart of the village was close to the graveyard and the inhabitants had gathered around a roughly hewn table under a huge tree. A simple meal of flatbread and water was brought out as dusk began to settle.

Tom tore a strip off the bread and tried to chew it. It had more sand than flour to it. He gulped down his water to force the bread down. He didn't want to insult the villagers, and they were looking at his every move.

"Don't you think you should eat something, Amelia?" Elenna whispered. "You'll offend them if you don't."

Amelia held up the battle-axe she was sharpening, the last rays of sun catching the blade. Then she

frowned at the bread and water. "I
have my own food." She beckoned to
Dray and he fished into his sack and
brought out a roasted chicken, an
apple and some cheese.

"Now that's what I call a meal,"
Amelia said smugly.

Tom's stomach rumbled in

response and Amelia's smile got
wider as she bit into a chicken leg.
Dray looked straight ahead, clearly
not interested in food at all.

Tom ground his teeth, annoyed
that his stomach had betrayed him.
It didn't seem right that Amelia had
all these extra provisions. *Is that*

even within the rules of the trial?

"Dray, get me some bread to go with this chicken, will you?" Amelia demanded with a little belch.

Dray delved into the sack once again. As he brought out a very fresh-looking loaf of bread, something round and shiny fell to the ground.

Tom recognised it instantly. It was his compass with its arrow that either pointed to *Destiny* or *Danger*. "Hey! That's mine."

Amelia abandoned her chicken and scrambled to pick up the compass.

"It's nothing," she insisted.

"You thief!" Elenna was on her

feet. "That compass belongs to Tom."

"I didn't steal it," Amelia said, her cheeks red. "I found it when I was looking for my sleeping quarters in King Hugo's palace."

Tom clenched his fists. "That compass was left in my chamber

and you know it," he snapped. "That's how you managed to avoid the bats – it showed you a safe path. You're a thief and chea—"

Tom broke off as a bell began to ring across the town.

Instantly, the villagers around the table threw down their food and began to race back to their homes. Karil turned to them. "I wish you the best of luck. I hope we only have to bury one of you." He then turned and ran towards his house.

Soon the village square was deserted. Just Tom, Amelia and their companions stood by the giant tree.

"So, what now?" said Amelia, placing her hands on her hips. But

Tom could see she was trembling a little.

A terrible screech cut through the semi-darkness. Tom drew his sword.

Looking up, he saw a winged silhouette pass over the moon, then vanish behind some clouds.

"Krytor is coming," he said.

6

THE BLOOD BAT

The giant bat dived downwards, his large head and wide, flat face illuminated by the moon's silvery light. His massive leathery wings would have spanned King Hugo's throne room, but he swooped and swirled easily, the reddish fur on his powerful body rippling in the wind.

With a screech, the blood bat folded his wings back and sped straight towards Tom and his companions. Tom was faster, though. He grabbed Elenna and yanked them both to the ground.

As they tumbled across the rough earth, Tom could smell a musty stink and, looking up, he saw the Beast's furry belly and the gleam of razor-sharp talons glinting past. Krytor began to circle them and Tom could see the slash of the bat's mouth and a protruding tongue.

Amelia and Dray were still on their feet. The older girl swung her battle-axe above her head. "Come and get me, if you dare," she cried.

"You filthy flying rodent."

Krytor wheeled in the sky and surged towards her with a piercing cry. He swiped out viciously with his talons.

"Watch out!" Tom cried.

Amelia ducked, only just saving her head, but Krytor knocked her battle-axe from her hands with a powerful swipe of his talons. The weapon clattered to the ground and, for a moment, Amelia looked utterly shocked and terrified.

Then Dray was in front of her. He drew his massive broadsword with both hands and shielded Amelia, his face as still and stony as the mountains.

Krytor was still hovering in
the air, as if working out the best
way to attack. The sound of his
massive wingbeats filled the night,
making everything shudder, but

Dray did not flinch.

He may be prepared to fight to the death for his niece, Tom thought, *but he's not going to be fast enough with such a large broadsword. I need to do something.*

"Get under the cover of that tree," Tom told Elenna. "Krytor will find it harder to get to you under there."

"Where are you going?" Elenna asked. "I'm coming with you."

"No, I need you to cover me."

Elenna nodded reluctantly and readied an arrow.

Tom ran across the village square. He could hear the bat's wingbeats following him and the *twang* of Elenna's bowstring as she let her arrows fly at the Beast.

Tom leapt up onto one of the domed roofs of the mud huts. The Beast was right on top of him. He could feel the hot, fetid breath on his neck.

Tom met Krytor's outstretched talons with the edge of his blade. There was a shower of sparks and the force of the impact threw Tom onto his back. He lay there stunned for a moment. Every part of his body ached and Tom realised how vulnerable he was without the power of the Golden Armour.

"Surely now is not the time for a rest," Amelia called up.

Tom grimaced. Standing up once more, he surveyed the village. He spotted the giant bat straight away. He had flown away to land on the tiled roof of a barn-like building. One of his talons looked broken and ragged from Tom's blow.

Grunting with effort, Amelia hurled a rock at the Beast and hit his flank.

Krytor roared at Amelia in fury and spread his wings, ready to attack once more.

Tom somersaulted off the roof and came to stand in front of Amelia. However brave the other contender pretended to be, he'd seen the fear on her face when Krytor had knocked the battle-axe from her hand.

"Stay back," Tom said. "I'll handle this." He expected some kind of furious response. But there was none. He swiftly turned his head and saw that she'd vanished already.

Where had she gone?

Tom turned back to Krytor – the Beast had not left the tiled roof and was studying him with strange red eyes. Then Tom saw Amelia. She had climbed up onto the building's stone roof and now stood directly behind the Beast.

Her eyes glittered with excitement as she raised her battle-axe.

"No, stop!" Tom cried, but it was too late. Amelia's weapon hacked into Krytor's leathery wing. The Beast gave a screech of pain and viciously swatted Amelia off the roof. Tom saw her tumble to the ground and lie still. Krytor thrashed his ruined wing, hissing in agony.

"Cover me!" Tom shouted to Elenna.

He ran towards Amelia's motionless form as arrows shot overhead. Krytor's fur deflected them, but at least Elenna was keeping the Beast busy. Tom knelt over Amelia, checking the pulse in her neck. She was still breathing.

"Tom, watch out!" cried Elenna. Looking up he saw that Krytor, even under the hail of arrows, had now managed to spread both his wings. The bat opened his mouth to reveal fangs dripping with foul-smelling saliva, and dived off the roof towards them.

Tom thrust out his shield as a

battering ram to drive back the
Beast, his shoulder staining against
the hammering claws. *Where is
Dray?* Tom wondered. *We need his*

help. The bat ripped the shield free from Tom's arm and dashed it to the ground.

With only his sword to protect him, Tom slashed out but the Beast charged into his side, knocking him

to the ground. Tom expected sharp
fangs to rip into him at any moment
but then heard the whistle of an
arrow. Krytor staggered backwards,
a shaft sticking out of his wing.

Tom took his chance. He dived for

his shield and leapt to his feet.

He whirled round to face the Beast but Krytor had launched himself into the air again and was staring down at the still unconscious Amelia.

Tom felt a flash of anger. Why hasn't Dray moved Amelia to safety?

Amelia's uncle was standing nearby, as still as a statue, doing nothing.

"Dray, get Amelia," Tom ordered. "I'll distract the Beast."

Dray continued to stand motionless.

What is his problem? Tom wondered with frustration. *If he really is Amelia's uncle, he doesn't seem very concerned about her.*

The Beast circled Tom and Amelia but a flurry of Elenna's arrows stopped Krytor from getting any closer. *But how many arrows has she got left?* Tom wondered. *There can't be many.*

Amelia groaned and put a hand to her head as she began to wake up. Tom stared up at the Beast. Fighting him on the ground was not working. If only he could get on Krytor's back, then maybe he could do a better job of subduing him.

I'll need some rope, Tom thought. He turned to Elenna and called out his plan. His friend nodded and

broke her cover from the canopy
of the big tree to get Tom what he
needed.

Turning back to face the Beast,
Tom saw that Amelia was now on
her feet and had run into the nearby
graveyard with Dray by her side.

The Beast took off in pursuit and
Tom followed.

As the Beast landed on the ground,
Amelia ducked behind one of the tall
tombstones. "Attack," she ordered
Dray.

Her uncle swung his sword in
dizzying arcs as he approached the
Beast.

Tom winced. There was power
in Dray's swordsmanship, but no

accuracy. *He's going to get himself killed.*

At that moment, Krytor dipped his head and charged forwards. He butted into Dray, knocking the sword from his grip and sending it spinning across the ground.

Blinking his shining yellow eyes, the Beast stalked over to Dray and lifted a clawed foot, ready to tear him to pieces.

7

MAGIC FLUTE

Tom did the only thing he could think of to close the distance. He hurled his shield at Krytor. It flew through the air and struck the Beast on the side of his furry head.

The giant bat shook his muzzle as he took a staggering step forward. Dray only just managed to roll out of the way.

Dazed, Krytor stumbled about and smashed apart the fences that lay between the graveyard and the village huts. Tom had begun to approach when, out of the corner of his eye, he spotted that a door to one of the huts was slightly ajar. He caught a glimpse of a familiar face peering out at them. It was

Karil with his wooden flute around his neck.

The flute, Tom thought. *Karil used it before to scare away many bats. Is it possible that the flute might work on Krytor?*

Tom raced over to the hut. "Karil, please let me borrow your flute."

The boy nodded and was about to untie it when his father appeared.

"This is not our fight," Karil's father snapped, and dragged his son back into the hut and slammed the door behind him.

Tom punched a fist into his palm in frustration. Then Elenna appeared at his side, a length of rope looped over her shoulder –

she'd already lassoed the end.

Dray was dragging himself up behind one of the tombstones, but Amelia was on the attack again, swinging her axe at Krytor and driving him back. The Beast was still disoriented and bumped against one of the mud huts, shaking it to its foundations.

"Amelia, be careful," Tom shouted. "There are innocent people inside there. They'll get hurt."

"They're not my problem," Amelia retorted. "No room for mercy if I'm going to succeed in this trial."

Raising the battle-axe above her head, she charged towards the Beast. Dray joined her as well, his broadsword slashing down in wide arcs. Krytor spread his two damaged wings and propelled himself upwards. The blast of air knocked both Dray and Amelia off their feet.

But Elenna's lasso caught one of the Beast's claws.

The blood bat gave a cry of rage and shot up in the air, dragging the rope out of Elenna's hands. Tom leapt after it, snatching at the end. He gritted his teeth and held on to the rope as it tried to race through his grip. The twined length cut into his palm and burnt his fingers, but Tom didn't let go – even as he felt his feet leave the ground.

Krytor rose higher and higher
but then gave another shriek of
anger as he realised that Tom was
an unwanted passenger. The Beast
dived downwards, and tried to

smash Tom into the roof of the huts. Tom curled his body upwards just in time.

Krytor climbed back in the sky until he was over the graveyard once more and Tom could see the empty grave below. *Not today,* Tom vowed. *I'm going to survive this trial.*

Up ahead, he saw Amelia scrambling onto the roof of one of the huts. The Beast immediately changed direction and headed straight for her. *Now that's someone with a death wish,* Tom thought to himself. Still, he knew that he couldn't allow her to face the Beast alone.

As they closed in on Amelia, Tom yanked hard on the rope to make Krytor veer off target.

They shot past, and Tom looked back at the roof. Amelia wasn't there. *Did she fall off?* He hadn't heard her scream but he couldn't know for sure if he'd managed to avoid Amelia completely.

Tom shook his head. The Beast needed to be stopped. He heaved himself up the rope, arms burning.

Krytor no longer seemed interested in smashing Tom into the huts down below. If anything, he was flying much higher than before. As Tom neared the top of the rope, he understood why.

Amelia was on the Beast's back! She must have leapt on as they shot past.

With her teeth gritted, her knees were astride the Beast's back as if she was riding a horse. Tom shook his head in amazement, admiring her courage despite himself. *It's exactly the sort of thing I might have done.*

"Amelia," Tom cried. "Help me up, and we can defeat this Beast together."

Amelia leant towards him and Tom thought she was about to hold out a hand when he noticed a glint in her eye.

Raising her axe, she brought it

down on the rope.

"No!" Tom cried,

She grinned as the rope began to fray. "Any good at flying, Tom?" she asked sweetly. "I think you're about to find out!"

CRASH LANDING!

"Amelia! Please!" Tom begged. "It doesn't have to be like this."

"I'm afraid it does." Amelia readied herself to cut at the fraying rope again. "Only one can win."

She raised her battle-axe but gave a cry as something sharp whizzed past her ear. She drew back in surprise.

Elenna, Tom realised with relief. Her arrow had saved him. He looked down and saw that his friend was waving up at him and she had something in her hand. It was Karil's flute!

Great, Tom thought. *But how am I going to get it?*

The question was left unanswered, as he heard something above him rip. As the rope gave way, he flung himself sideways and grabbed one of Krytor's talons. Dangling there, he watching the frayed rope float back to the ground.

It gave him an idea.

"Elenna," he cried, hoping his words would carry over the

distance. "Use your arrow and the rope to send me the flute. I'll catch—"

Tom broke off as his whole head began to rattle. Krytor was kicking his legs, trying to dislodge his hanger-on. Tom held on even more tightly and just hoped that Elenna had heard his request.

"No, no, no!" He heard Amelia cry from above. Krytor's shaking must have unseated her because the older girl slipped off the bat's back and went off the side. She swiftly grabbed a handful of the bat's fur and then reached out and grasped another of Krytor's talons.

Tom and Amelia faced each other

as they both hung below the Beast.

"The view isn't too bad from up here, is it?" Amelia mused.

"You tried to kill me," Tom said.

Amelia looked a little bit embarrassed. "I just want to win. I'm not going to be sorry about that and—"She broke off as the Beast gave a furious cry. He lowered his massive head and tried to snap at both of them with his fangs.

The smell of Krytor's breath was almost enough to make Tom gag, but he held on. With a spitting sound, the bat stopped snapping at them, folded his wings back and angled himself downwards instead.

"Oh, no," Amelia groaned. "He'll smash us to pieces."

Looking down at the fast-approaching ground, Tom saw that Elenna had lined up the flute on her bowstring. "Now!" he cried.

Elenna shot the instrument up at him, and Tom whipped out his free hand and caught it.

"Great, I can listen to music while I die," said Amelia.

Tom brought the flute to his lips and blew.

Our last chance...

Krytor reacted at once to the whistling sound. With a screech,

his folded wings unfurled and he
levelled into a glide, level with the
mud hut roofs.

Tom jumped clear of the Beast
and rolled across the ground. He
saw Amelia do the same. Krytor's
wing caught the edge of a building,
and with a shriek the Beast tipped

and rolled across the ground, throwing up a billow of mud and dust. He came to rest beside the graveyard.

"Tom, are you all right?" Elenna asked, rushing to his side and helping him up.

"I'm fine," Tom replied, rubbing at the bruises that were already developing on his arms. "Thanks for sending up that flute."

Elenna smiled. "We're a team, remember?"

Tom nodded. With Elenna by his side, he crept towards the Beast, who was lying quite still apart from the rise and fall of his breath. Tom drew his sword. "Submit," he ordered the blood bat. But as he got closer, he realised he did not need his sword. Krytor seemed much calmer now. The flute had subdued him. The Beast lay his head down in front of Tom in a gesture of surrender.

Tom wished he had the red jewel. There was much he wanted to say to the Beast. He sheathed his blade but, as he did so, Amelia appeared behind Krytor with Dray's huge sword in her hand.

"Amelia, don't," Tom cried, but it was too late. She plunged the sword through the Beast's back. Krytor slumped forwards, eyes closed.

"A win for me," Amelia crowed.

Tom shook his head in disgust. "You didn't need to do that. He'd surrendered!"

Villagers emerged from the huts, goggling at the Beast. But as they looked, Krytor's body began to vibrate, so fast that he was just a blur. Then he began to fade away

until he'd disappeared completely.

"The Beast is not dead," the shaman explained. "He will return when he is needed."

"What?" Amelia said. "Well, that was a waste of time!"

Tom felt a surge of relief and realised that they couldn't have

been the first warriors to have defeated Krytor. The blood bat had clearly lived several times.

Amelia sighed and gave the sword back to Dray. "Let's hope the others are just as easy. What's next?"

Tom rolled his eyes. She was just trying to sound tough, but he'd seen her tremble when Krytor first appeared.

"There's our answer," Elenna said. She was pointing to where the Beast had lain a moment ago. Thick black smoke was rising from the ground and spreading its tendrils. When it cleared, the black abyss was waiting for them.

"Excellent," Amelia said. "Dray

and I will continue with the trial
alone if you're too scared."

Tom looked at Elenna. He
realised now that on this Quest, it
wasn't only the Beasts who stood

in his way. Kara's descendant was formidable and ruthless.

Scared? Yes, of course he was. *Only a fool wouldn't be.*

But while there was blood in his veins, there was no turning back.

THE END

1

CONGRATULATIONS, YOU HAVE COMPLETED THIS QUEST!

At the end of each chapter you were awarded a special gold coin. The QUEST in this book was worth an amazing 8 coins.

Look at the Beast Quest totem picture inside the back cover of this book to see how far you've come in your journey to become

MASTER OF THE BEASTS.

The more books you read, the more coins you will collect!

Do you want your own
Beast Quest Totem?

1. Cut out and collect the coin below
2. Go to the Beast Quest website
3. Download and print out your totem
4. Add your coin to the totem
www.beastquest.co.uk/totem

Don't miss the next exciting Beast Quest book, SOARA THE STINGING SPECTRE!

Read on for a sneak peek...

THE OTHER SIDE OF THE ABYSS

Tom fell through silence, a thick, heavy nothingness pressing in on him from every side. He strained to see something – anything – but the blackness was so complete he might as well have been blind.

Then the opposite – white light flooding his vision. Tom threw up an arm to shield his eyes and blinked, struggling to focus in the sudden brightness. And, once he could, he found himself standing on a deserted beach gazing out at a perfectly clear sea. A moment later, Elenna stumbled to his side.

She shuddered, as if shaking away the touch of the abyss, then squinted into the glaring sun. "What is this place?" she asked.

Tom shrugged. He'd never seen anywhere like it. Powdery grey sand stretched away on either side and led down to the water's edge. The sea was still and silent, its smooth surface as transparent as glass. Lilac clouds scudded across a purple sky above them at an impossible speed, but Tom couldn't feel the faintest breeze on his skin.

"I think we've reached stage two of the Trial of Heroes," he said.

"Hey! Stop gawking and get out of my way!" a female voice blurted behind them. "I've got a Beast to kill!" Elbows shoved Tom and Elenna aside and Amelia barged past, closely followed by Dray, her silent, hulking uncle.

Amelia put her hands on her hips and gazed out at the strange, flat landscape. "So, I guess it's a race to the next Beast, then," she said, her blustery tone tinged with unease.

About time she began to realise this isn't a game! Tom thought.

Amelia drew a compass from her pocket and turned her back, blocking Tom and Elenna's view of the device.

Tom clenched his teeth. "If you don't want to get disqualified for cheating," he said, "you'd better let us all use that compass."

Amelia's broad shoulders tensed and Tom knew he'd hit a nerve. Despite all Tom had done for Avantia, as a direct descendent of Kara the Fearless, Amelia had as much right to the title of Master of the Beasts as he did. Tom had given up his jewelled belt and

magical armour when he'd agreed
to undertake the Trial of Heroes,
on which two rivals raced to find
the mythical Rune of Courage in an
enchanted realm called the Nowhere
Lands. By the rules of the trial,
Amelia should have brought no
magical artefacts either, but she had
somehow managed to sneak out with
Tom's compass.

Amelia shrugged and turned.
"Fine," she said, holding the compass
out before her. "It won't make any
difference – I'll still win because I'm
the rightful Mistress of the Beasts."

Tom and Elenna exchanged an
exasperated look, then craned over
the compass in Amelia's hand.

Amelia moved the compass slowly
over the landscape, pointing first
along the empty beach to their
left. The compass needle didn't so

much as twitch. Amelia turned, and Tom and Elenna turned with her, watching the compass closely as Amelia ran it along the beach to their right. Still nothing. Finally, Amelia turned to face the motionless sea. She held the compass towards a small, steep-sided island carpeted with dark green, lush vegetation. A narrow grey beach ringed the island's forested cliffs. The compass needle swung slowly between *Destiny* and *Danger*. Amelia stopped, frowning at the island.

"It looks like we need to get out there somehow," Elenna said.

"I wouldn't recommend it." A voice like a rusty hinge spoke

from behind them.

Tom turned to see a lean, bow-legged woman grinning at him from a wrinkled, sun-browned face. Skinny arms and legs stuck like knobbly twigs from the woman's woven grass tunic, and a halo of white hair stood out from her head. Bracelets threaded with what looked like the delicate bones of small birds decorated her wrists and ankles, and she carried a long bone spear. One of her pupils was misted white but her eyes glittered as they scanned Tom's face.

"You think it's a bad idea?" Tom said.

The old woman's gap-toothed grin

broadened and she lifted her hands, the gnarled fingers curled like claws. "The strange ones live there," she said, eyes swivelling madly. "They don't like visitors." She dropped her hands, and shrugged. "Why not stay here instead? I'll make you some tea."

Tom shook his head, wondering if this woman was part of the trial – a way to stop them succeeding. "I'm afraid we have to get to that island." He glanced again at the forested cliffs, worry gnawing at his belly. *The strange ones? Could they be in league with the Beast?* Elenna shot him an uneasy look.

"I'm not afraid of a few islanders," Amelia said, hefting her axe. The old woman chuckled.

"Is that so?" she said. "That must be nice for you. But only a fool lives without fear."

Read
SOARA THE STINGING SPECTRE
to find out what happens next!

FIGHT THE BEASTS,
FEAR THE MAGIC

Are you a BEAST QUEST mega fan?
Do you want to know about all the latest news,
competitions and books before anyone else?

Then join our Quest Club!

Visit the BEAST QUEST website
and sign up today!

www.beastquest.co.uk

Discover the new Beast Quest mobile game from

Available free on iOS and Android

Available on **iTunes**   GET IT ON **Google** play   **amazon**.com

Guide Tom on his Quest to free the Good Beasts
of Avantia from Malvel's evil spells.

Battle the Beasts, defeat the minions,
unearth the secrets and collect
rewards as you journey through the
Kingdom of Avantia.

31901064428305

DOW BEGIN THE ADVENTURE NOW!